To Jane Chapman, an artist whose illustrations
are like a Christmas gift to this author—thanks.
Bear and his friends say thank you as well.
—K. W.

For Mum and Dad (who stayed
up for Matt, Sally, and me!)
—J. C.

Margaret K. McElderry Books
An imprint of Simon & Schuster Children's Publishing Division
1230 Avenue of the Americas
New York, New York 10020

The text of this book is set in Adobe Caslon.
The illustrations were rendered in acrylic paint.

Manufactured in China

2 4 6 8 10 9 7 5 3 1

Library of Congress Cataloging-in-Publication Data
Wilson, Karma.
Bear stays up for Christmas / Karma Wilson ; illustrations by Jane Chapman.
p. cm.
Summary: Bear's friends awaken him the day before Christmas and help him to stay awake as they bake fruitcakes,
fill stockings, and sing carols; then, while they sleep, he prepares his own surprise.
ISBN 0-689-85278-9
[1. Bears—Fiction. 2. Christmas—Fiction. 3. Forest animals—Fiction.
4. Stories in rhyme.] I. Chapman, Jane, 1970- ill. II. Title.
PZ8.3.W6976Bet 2004
[E]—dc21
2002151867

Bear Stays Up
FOR CHRISTMAS

Karma Wilson

illustrations by Jane Chapman

MARGARET K. MCELDERRY BOOKS

New York   London   Toronto   Sydney

The day before Christmas,
snuggled on his floor,
Bear sleeps soundly
with a great big snore.

"Dear Bear, GET UP!"
Mouse shouts in his ear.
"We won't let you sleep
through Christmas this year."

His friends are all there, gathered in his lair . . .

and the bear
wakes
up.

He stands with a stretch
and a great big sigh.
"I hope I can make it.
I do want to try."

"Don't worry," squeaks Mouse.
Hare says, "It's all right.
We'll keep you busy
all day and all night."

He tries to lie down,
but his friends all frown . . .

so the bear
stays
up.

"Come on," says Badger,
"time to follow me.
In Pine Grove Glen
there's a fine Christmas tree."

So they stomp through the woods
and they tromp down the track.
They hoist up the tree
onto Bear's big back.

He plods very slow
as they trudge through the snow.

But
the bear
stays up.

Back at the cave
Gopher brews mint tea
and Mole pops corn
to string upon the tree.

Raven and Wren
bake a fresh fruitcake.
The friends do their best
to keep Bear awake.

His shoulders start to stoop and his eyelids droop.

But the bear
stays
up.

They hang up their stockings
by warm firelight
and hum Christmas songs
like "O Holy Night."

They cuddle and sing
as they wait for the sun. . . .

But soon all the voices
fade to just one.
A bright star glows
while his good friends doze . . .

but the bear
stays
up!

Bear giggles and grins.
He works and he wraps.
He bustles and bakes
while everyone naps.

He piles up presents
under the tree.
But who's at the doorway?
Bear doesn't see. . . .

He toils all night
until the sun rises,
making his friends
their Christmas surprises!

Just before dawn he lets out a yawn . . .

but he still
stays
up.

When Christmas arrives,
so lovely and white,
Bear's friends awake
to a glorious sight.

Presents and goodies
are piled up tall.
"I stayed up," says Bear,
"just to share with you all."

As his friends shout with glee, Bear lies by the tree . . .

but he still
stays
up.

Wren flies to the stockings
and tweets out a cheer.
"Besides our bear's presents,
Santa was here!"

When all gifts are opened,
there's one last surprise.
Badger shows Bear
a quilt just his size.

Bear snuggles up tight and mutters, "Good night . . ."

Then Bear
falls
asleep.

His friends tidy up
and slip from the lair.
They whisper, "Sweet dreams.
Merry Christmas, dear Bear."